John Taylor

The Pennyles

Outlook

John Taylor

The Pennyles

1. Auflage | ISBN: 978-3-73262-694-6

Erscheinungsort: Frankfurt am Main, Deutschland

Erscheinungsjahr: 2018

Outlook Verlag GmbH, Frankfurt.

John Taylor

The Pennyles

Outlook

THE

PENNYLES

PILGRIMAGE,

OR

The Money-lesse perambulation,

of J<small>OHN</small> T<small>AYLOR</small>, *Alias*
the Kings Majesties
Water-Poet.

HOW HE TRAVAILED ON FOOT

from *London* to *Edenborough* in *Scotland*, not carrying
any Money to or fro, neither Begging, Borrowing,
or Asking Meate, drinke or
Lodging.

With his Description of his Entertainment

in all places of his Journey, and a true Report
of the unmatchable Hunting in the *Brea*
of *Marre* and *Badenoch* in
Scotland.

With other Observations, some serious and
worthy of Memory, and some merry
and not hurtfull to be Remembred.

Lastly that (which is Rare in a Travailer)
all is true.

LONDON

Printed by *Edw: Allde*, at the charges of the
Author. 1618

T<small>O THE</small> T<small>RULY</small>
N<small>OBLE AND</small> R<small>IGHT</small>

1

Honorable Lord GEORGE MARQUIS
of Buckingham, Viscount Villiers, Baron of
Whaddon, Justice in Eyre of all his Majesty's
Forests, Parks, and Chases beyond Trent, Master
of the Horse to his Majesty, and one of the Gentlemen
of his Highness Royal Bed-Chamber, Knight
of the most Noble Order of the Garter, and
one of his Majesty's most Honorable
Privy Council of both the
Kingdoms of England
and Scotland.

ight Honorable, and worthy honoured Lord, as in my Travels, I was entertained, welcomed, and relieved by many Honourable Lords, Worshipful Knights, Esquires, Gentlemen, and others both in England and Scotland. So now your Lordship's inclination hath incited, or invited my poor muse to shelter herself under the shadow of your honorable patronage, not that there is any worth at all in my sterile invention, but in all humility I acknowledge that it is only your Lordship's acceptance, that is able to make this nothing, something, and withal engage me ever.

Your Honors,
In all observance,
JOHN TAYLOR.

TO ALL MY LOVING ADVENTURERS, BY WHAT NAME OR TITLE SOEVER, MY GENERAL SALUTATION.

eader, these Travels of mine into Scotland, *were not undertaken, neither in imitation, or emulation of any man, but only devised by myself, on purpose to make trial of my friends both in this Kingdom of* England, *and that of* Scotland, *and because I would be an eye-witness of divers things which I had heard of that Country; and whereas many shallow-brained Critics, do lay an aspersion on me, that I was set on by others, or that I did undergo this project, either in malice, or mockage of Master* Benjamin Jonson, *I vow by the faith of a Christian, that their imaginations are all wide, for he is a gentleman, to whom I am so much obliged for many undeserved courtesies that I have received from him, and from others by his favour, that I durst never to be so impudent or ungrateful, as either to suffer any man's persuasions, or mine own instigation, to incite me, to make so bad a requital, for so much goodness formerly received; so much for that, and now Reader, if you expect*

> That I should write of cities' situations,
> Or that of countries I should make relations:
> Of brooks, crooks, nooks; of rivers, bournes and rills,
> Of mountains, fountains, castles, towers and hills,
> Of shires, and piers, and memorable things,
> Of lives and deaths of great commanding kings,
> I touch not those, they not belong to me;
> But if such things as these you long to see,
> Lay down my book, and but vouchsafe to read
> The learned *Camden*, or laborious *Speed*.

> *And so God speed you and me, whilst I rest*
> *Yours in all thankfulness:*
> JOHN TAYLOR.

TAYLOR'S
PENNILESS PILGRIMAGE.

ist Lordlings, list (if you have lust to list)
I write not here a tale of had I wist:
But you shall hear of travels, and relations,
Descriptions of strange (yet English) fashions.
And he that not believes what here is writ,
Let him (as I have done) make proof of it.
The year of grace, accounted (as I ween)
One thousand twice three hundred and eighteen,
And to relate all things in order duly,
'Twas Tuesday last, the fourteenth day of July,
Saint *Revels* day, the almanack will tell ye
The sign in *Virgo* was, or near the belly:
The moon full three days old, the wind full south;
At these times I began this trick of youth.
I speak not of the tide, for understand,
My legs I made my oars, and rowed by land,
Though in the morning I began to go
Good fellows trooping, flocked me so,
That make what haste I could, the sun was set,
E're from the gates of *London* I could get.
At last I took my latest leave thus late,
At the Bell Inn, that's *extra Aldersgate*.
There stood a horse that my provant[1] should carry,
From that place to the end of my fegary,[2]
My horse no horse, or mare, but gelded nag,
That with good understanding bore my bag:
And of good carriage he himself did show,

These things are excellent in a beast you know.
There in my knapsack, (to pay hunger's fees)
I had good bacon, biscuit, neat's-tongue, cheese
With roses, barberries, of each conserves,
And mithridate, that vigorous health perserves:
And I entreat you take these words for no-lies,
I had good *Aqua vitæ, Rosa* so-lies:
With sweet *Ambrosia*, (the gods' own drink)
Most excellent gear for mortals, as I think,
Besides, I had both vinegar and oil,
That could a daring saucy stomach foil.
This foresaid Tuesday night 'twixt eight and nine,
Well rigged and ballasted, both with beer and wine,
I stumbling forward, thus my jaunt begun,
And went that night as far as *Islington*.
There did I find (I dare affirm it bold)
A Maidenhead of twenty-five years old,
But surely it was painted, like a whore,
And for a sign, or wonder, hanged at door,
Which shows a Maidenhead, that's kept so long,
May be hanged up, and yet sustain no wrong.
There did my loving friendly host begin
To entertain me freely to his inn:
And there my friends, and good associates,
Each one to mirth himself accommodates.
At Well-head both for welcome, and for cheer,
Having a good *New ton*, of good stale beer:
There did we *Trundle*[3] down health, after health,
(Which oftentimes impairs both health and wealth.)
Till everyone had filled his mortal trunk,
And only *No-body*[3] was three parts drunk.
The morrow next, Wednesday Saint *Swithin's* day,
From ancient *Islington* I took my way.
At *Holywell* I was enforced carouse,
Ale high, and mighty, at the Blindman's House.
But there's a help to make amends for all,
That though the ale be great, the pots be small.
At *Highgate* Hill to a strange house I went,
And saw the people were to eating bent,
In either borrowed, craved, asked, begged, or bought,
But most laborious with my teeth I wrought.
I did not this, 'cause meat or drink was scant,

But I did practise thus before my want;
Like to a Tilter that would win the prize,
Before the day he'll often exercise.
So I began to put in use, at first
These principles 'gainst hunger, 'gainst thirst.
Close to the Gate,[4] there dwelt a worthy man,
That well could take his whiff, and quaff his can,
Right Robin Good-fellow, but humours evil,
Do call him *Robin Pluto*, or the devil.
But finding him a devil, freely hearted,
With friendly farewells I took leave and parted,
And as alongst I did my journey take,
I drank at *Broom's well*, for pure fashion's sake,
Two miles I travelled then without a bait,
The Saracen's Head at *Whetstone* entering straight,
I found an host, that might lead an host of men,
Exceeding fat, yet named *Lean*, and *Fen*.[5]
And though we make small reckoning of him here,
He's known to be a very great man there.
There I took leave of all my company,
Bade all farewell, yet spake to *No-body*.
Good reader think not strange, what I compile,
For *No-body* was with me all this while.
And *No-body* did drink, and, wink, and scink,
And on occasion freely spent his chink.
If anyone desire to know the man,
Walk, stumble, *Trundle*, but in *Barbican*.
There's as good beer and ale as ever twang'd,
And in that street kind *No-body*[6] is hanged.
But leaving him unto his matchless fame,
I to St. *Albans* in the evening came,
Where Master *Taylor*, at the Saracen's Head,
Unasked (unpaid for) me both lodged and fed.
The tapsters, hostlers, chamberlains, and all,
Saved me a labour, that I need not call,
The jugs were filled and filled, the cups went round,
And in a word great kindness there I found,
For which both to my cousin, and his men,
I'll still be thankful in word, deed, and pen.
Till Thursday morning there I made my stay,
And then I went plain *Dunstable* highway.

My very heart with drought methought did shrink,
I went twelve miles, and no one bade me drink.
Which made me call to mind, that instant time,
That drunkenness was a most sinful crime.
When *Puddle-hill* I footed down, and past
A mile from thence, I found a hedge at last.
There stroke we sail, our bacon, cheese, and bread,
We drew like fiddlers, and like farmers fed.
And whilst two hours we there did take our ease,
My nag made shift to mump green pulse[7] and peas.
Thus we our hungry stomachs did supply,
And drank the water of a brook hard by.
Away toward *Hockley* in the Hole, we make,
When straight a horseman did me overtake,
Who knew me, and would fain have given me coin,
I said, my bonds did me from coin enjoin,
I thanked and prayed him to put up his chink,
And willingly I wished it drowned in drink.
Away rode he, but like an honest man,
I found at *Hockley* standing at the Swan,
A formal tapster, with a jug and glass,
Who did arrest me: I most willing was
To try the action, and straight put in bail,
My fees were paid before, with sixpence ale,
To quit this kindness, I most willing am,
The man that paid for all, his name is *Dam*,
At the Green Dragon, against *Grays-Inn* gate,
He lives in good repute, and honest state.
I forward went in this my roving race,
To *Stony Stratford* I toward night did pace,
My mind was fixed through the town to pass,
To find some lodging in the hay or grass,
But at the *Queen's Arms*, from the window there,
A comfortable voice I chanced to hear,
Call *Taylor, Taylor*, and be hanged come hither,
I looked for small entreaty and went thither,
There were some friends, which I was glad to see,
Who knew my journey; lodged, and boarded me.
On Friday morn, as I would take my way,
My friendly host entreated me to stay,
Because it rained, he told me I should have
Meat, drink, and horse-meat and not pay or crave.

I thanked him, and for his love remain his debtor,
But if I live, I will requite him better.
(From *Stony Stratford*) the way hard with stones,
Did founder me, and vex me to the bones.
In blustering weather, both for wind and rain,
Through *Towcester* I trotted with much pain,
Two miles from thence, we sat us down and dined,
Well bulwarked by a hedge, from rain and wind.
We having fed, away incontinent,
With weary pace toward *Daventry* we went.
Four miles short of it, one o'ertook me there,
And told me he would leave a jug of beer,
At *Daventry* at the Horse-shoe for my use.
I thought it no good manners to refuse,
But thanked him, for his kind unasked gift,
Whilst I was lame as scarce a leg could lift,
Came limping after to that stony town,
Whose hard streets made me almost halt right down.
There had my friend performed the words he said,
And at the door a jug of liquor staid,
The folks were all informed, before I came,
How, and wherefore my journey I did frame,
Which caused mine hostess from her door come out,
(Having a great wart rampant on her snout.)
The tapsters, hostlers, one another call,
The chamberlains with admiration all,
Were filled with wonder, more than wonderful,
As if some monster sent from the *Mogul*,
Some elephant from *Africa*, I had been,
Or some strange beast from the *Amazonian* Queen.
As buzzards, widgeons, woodcocks, and such fowl,
Do gaze and wonder at the broad-faced owl,
So did these brainless asses, all amazed,
With admirable *Nonsense* talked and gazed,
They knew my state (although not told by me)
That I could scarcely go, they all could see,
They drank of my beer, that to me was given,
But gave me not a drop to make all even,
And that which in my mind was most amiss,
My hostess she stood by and saw all this,
Had she but said, come near the house my friend,
For this day here shall be your journey's end.

9

Then had she done the thing which [she] did not,
And I in kinder words had paid the shot.
I do entreat my friends, (as I have some)
If they to *Daventry* do chance to come,
That they will baulk that inn; or if by chance,
Or accident into that house they glance,
Kind gentlemen, as they by you reap profit,
My hostess care of me, pray tell her of it,[8]
Yet do not neither; lodge there when you will,
You for your money shall be welcome still.
From thence that night, although my bones were sore,
I made a shift to hobble seven miles more:
The way to *Dunchurch*, foul with dirt and mire,
Able, I think, both man and horse to tire.
On *Dunsmoor* Heath, a hedge doth there enclose
Grounds, on the right hand, there I did repose.
Wit's whetstone, Want, there made us quickly learn,
With knives to cut down rushes, and green fern,
Of which we made a field-bed in the field,
Which sleep, and rest, and much content did yield.
There with my mother earth, I thought it fit
To lodge, and yet no incest did commit:
My bed was curtained with good wholesome airs,
And being weary, I went up no stairs:
The sky my canopy, bright *Phœbe* shined
Sweet bawling *Zephyrus* breathed gentle wind,
In heaven's star-chamber I did lodge that night,
Ten thousand stars, me to my bed did light;
There barricadoed with a bank lay we
Below the lofty branches of a tree,
There my bed-fellows and companions were,
My man, my horse, a bull, four cows, two steer:
But yet for all this most confused rout,
We had no bed-staves, yet we fell not out.
Thus nature, like an ancient free upholster,
Did furnish us with bedstead, bed, and bolster;
And the kind skies, (for which high heaven be thanked,)
Allowed us a large covering and a blanket;
Auroras face 'gan light our lodging dark,
We arose and mounted, with the mounting lark,
Through plashes, puddles, thick, thin, wet and dry,
I travelled to the city *Coventry*.

There Master Doctor *Holland*[9] caused me stay
The day of *Saturn* and the Sabbath day.
Most friendly welcome, he me did afford,
I was so entertained at bed and board,
Which as I dare not brag how much it was,
I dare not be ingrate and let it pass,
But with thanks many I remember it,
(Instead of his good deeds) in words and writ,
He used me like his son, more than a friend,
And he on Monday his commends did send
To *Newhall*, where a gentleman did dwell,
Who by his name is hight *Sacheverell*.
The Tuesday *July's* one and twentieth day,
I to the city *Lichfield* took my way,
At *Sutton Coldfield* with some friends I met,
And much ado I had from thence to get,
There I was almost put unto my trumps,
My horse's shoes were worn as thin as pumps;
But noble *Vulcan*, a mad smuggy smith,
All reparations me did furnish with.
The shoes were well removed, my palfrey shod,
And he referred the payment unto God.
I found a friend, when I to *Lichfield* came,
A joiner, and *John Piddock* is his name.
He made me welcome, for he knew my jaunt,
And he did furnish me with good provant:
He offered me some money, I refused it,
And so I took my leave, with thanks excused it,
That Wednesday, I a weary way did pass,
Rain, wind, stones, dirt, and dabbling dewy grass,
With here and there a pelting scattered village,
Which yielded me no charity, or pillage:
For all the day, nor yet the night that followed.
One drop of drink I'm sure my gullet swallowed.
At night I came to a stony town called *Stone*.
Where I knew none, nor was I known of none:
I therefore through the streets held on my pace,
Some two miles farther to some resting place:
At last I spied a meadow newly mowed,
The hay was rotten, the ground half o'erflowed:
We made a breach, and entered horse and man,
There our pavilion, we to pitch began,

Which we erected with green broom and hay,
To expel the cold, and keep the rain away;
The sky all muffled in a cloud 'gan lower,
And presently there fell a mighty shower,
Which without intermission down did pour,
From ten a night, until the morning's four.
We all that time close in our couch did lie,
Which being well compacted kept us dry.
The worst was, we did neither sup nor sleep,
And so a temperate diet we did keep.
The morning all enrobed in drifting fogs,
We being as ready as we had been dogs:
We need not stand upon long ready making,
But gaping, stretching, and our ears well shaking:
And for I found my host and hostess kind,
I like a true man left my sheets behind.
That Thursday morn, my weary course I framed,
Unto a town that is *Newcastle* named.
(Not that *Newcastle* standing upon *Tyne*)
But this town situation doth confine
Near *Cheshire*, in the famous county *Stafford*,
And for their love, I owe them not a straw for't;
    But now my versing muse craves some repose,
    And whilst she sleeps I'll spout a little prose.

In this town of *Newcastle*, I overtook an hostler, and I asked him what the next town was called, that was in my way toward *Lancaster*, he holding the end of a riding rod in his mouth, as if it had been a flute, piped me this answer, and said, *Talk-on-the-Hill*; I asked him again what he said *Talk-on- the-Hill*: I demanded the third time, and the third time he answered me as he did before, *Talk-on-the-Hill*. I began to grow choleric, and asked him why he could not talk, or tell me my way as well there as on the hill; at last I was resolved, that the next town was four miles off me, and that the name of it was, *Talk-on-the-Hill*: I had not travelled above two miles farther: but my last night's supper (which was as much as nothing) my mind being informed of it by my stomach. I made a virtue of necessity, and went to breakfast in the Sun: I have fared better at three Suns many times before now, in *Aldersgate Street*, *Cripplegate*, and new *Fish Street*; but here is the odds, at those Suns they will come upon a man with a tavern bill as sharp cutting as a tailor's bill of items: a watchman's-bill, or a welsh-hook falls not half so heavy upon a man; besides, most of the vintners have the law in their own hands, and have all their actions, cases, bills of debt, and such reckonings tried at their own bars;

from whence there is no appeal. But leaving these impertinences, in the material Sunshine, we eat a substantial dinner, and like miserable guests we did budget up the reversions.

> And now with sleep my muse hath eased her brain
> I'll turn my style from prose, to verse again.
> That which we could not have, we freely spared,
> And wanting drink, most soberly we fared.
> We had great store of fowl (but 'twas foul way)
> And kindly every step entreats me stay,
> The clammy clay sometimes my heels would trip,
> One foot went forward, the other back would slip,
> This weary day, when I had almost past,
> I came unto Sir *Urian Leigh's* at last,
> At *Adlington*, near *Macclesfield* he doth dwell,
> Beloved, respected, and reputed well.
> Through his great love, my stay with him was fixed,
> From Thursday night, till noon on Monday next,
> At his own table I did daily eat,
> Whereat may be supposed, did want no meat,
> He would have given me gold or silver either,
> But I, with many thanks, received neither,
> And thus much without flattery I dare swear,
> He is a knight beloved far and near,
> First he's beloved of his God above,
> (Which love he loves to keep, beyond all love)
> Next with a wife and children he is blest,
> Each having God's fear planted in their breast.
> With fair demaines, revenue of good lands,
> He's fairly blessed by the Almighty's hands,
> And as he's happy in these outward things,
> So from his inward mind continual springs
> Fruits of devotion, deeds of piety,
> Good hospitable works of charity,
> Just in his actions, constant in his word,
> And one that won his honour with the sword,
> He's no carranto, cap'ring, carpet knight,
> But he knows when, and how to speak or fight,
> I cannot flatter him, say what I can,
> He's every way a complete gentleman.
> I write not this, for what he did to me,
> But what mine ears, and eyes did hear and see,

Nor do I pen this to enlarge his fame
But to make others imitate the same,
For like a trumpet were I pleased to blow,
I would his worthy worth more amply show,
But I already fear have been too bold,
And crave his pardon, me excused to hold.
Thanks to his sons and servants every one,
Both males and females all, excepting none.
To bear a letter he did me require,
Near *Manchester*, unto a good Esquire:
His kinsman *Edmund Prestwitch*, he ordained,
That I was at *Manchester* entertained
Two nights, and one day, ere we thence could pass,
For men and horse, roast, boiled, and oats, and grass;
This gentleman not only gave harbour,
But in the morning sent me to his barber,
Who laved, and shaved me, still I spared my purse,
Yet sure he left me many a hair the worse.
But in conclusion, when his work was ended,
His glass informed, my face was much amended.
And for the kindness he to me did show,
God grant his customers beards faster grow,
That though the time of year be dear or cheap,
From fruitful faces he may mow and reap.
Then came a smith, with shoes, and tooth and nail,
He searched my horse's hoofs, mending what did fail,
Yet this I note, my nag, through stones and dirt,
Did shift shoes twice, ere I did shift one shirt:
Can these kind things be in oblivion hid?
No, Master *Prestwitch*, this and much more did,
His friendship did command and freely gave
All before writ, and more than I durst crave.
But leaving him a little, I must tell,
How men of *Manchester* did use me well,
Their loves they on the tenter-hooks did rack,
Roast, boiled, baked, too—too—much, white, claret, sack,
Nothing they thought too heavy or too hot,
Can followed can, and pot succeeded pot,
That what they could do, all they thought too little,
Striving in love the traveller to whittle.
We went into the house of one *John Pinners*,

(A man that lives amongst a crew of sinners)
And there eight several sorts of ale we had,
All able to make one stark drunk or mad.
But I with courage bravely flinched not,
And gave the town leave to discharge the shot.
We had at one time set upon the table,
Good ale of hyssop, 'twas no Æsop-fable:
Then had we ale of sage, and ale of malt,
And ale of wormwood, that could make one halt,
With ale of rosemary, and betony,
And two ales more, or else I needs must lie.
But to conclude this drinking aley-tale,
We had a sort of ale, called scurvy ale.
Thus all these men, at their own charge and cost,
Did strive whose love should be expressed most,
And farther to declare their boundless loves,
They saw I wanted, and they gave me gloves,
In deed, and very deed, their loves were such,
That in their praise I cannot write too much;
They merit more than I have here compiled,
I lodged at the Eagle and the Child,
Whereas my hostess, (a good ancient woman)
Did entertain me with respect, not common.
She caused my linen, shirts, and bands be washed,
And on my way she caused me be refreshed,
She gave me twelve silk points, she gave me bacon,
Which by me much refused, at last was taken,
In troth she proved a mother unto me,
For which, I evermore will thankful be.
But when to mind these kindnesses I call,
Kind Master *Prestwitch* author is of all,
And yet Sir *Urian Leigh's* good commendation,
Was the main ground of this my recreation.
From both of them, there what I had, I had,
Or else my entertainment had been bad.
O all you worthy men of *Manchester*,
(True bred bloods of the County *Lancaster*)
When I forget what you to me have done,
Then let me headlong to confusion run.
To noble Master *Prestwitch* I must give
Thanks, upon thanks, as long as I do live,
His love was such, I ne'er can pay the score,

He far surpassed all that went before,
A horse and man he sent, with boundless bounty, To
bring me quite through *Lancaster's* large county,
Which I well know is fifty miles at large,
And he defrayed all the cost and charge.
This unlooked pleasure, was to me such pleasure,
That I can ne'er express my thanks with measure.
So Mistress *Saracoal*, hostess kind,
And *Manchester* with thanks I leftbehind.
The Wednesday being *July's* twenty nine,
My journey I to *Preston* did confine,
All the day long it rained but one shower,
Which from the morning to the evening did pour,
And I, before to *Preston* I could get,
Was soused, and pickled both with rain and sweat,
But there I was supplied with fire and food,
And anything I wanted sweet and good.
There, at the Hind, kind Master *Hind* mine host,
Kept a good table, baked and boiled, and roast,
There Wednesday, Thursday, Friday I did stay,
And hardly got from thence on Saturday.
Unto my lodging often did repair,
Kind Master *Thomas Banister*, the Mayor,
Who is of worship, and of good respect,
And in his charge discreet and circumspect.
For I protest to God I never saw,
A town more wisely governed by the law.
They told me when my Sovereign there was last,
That one man's rashness seemed to give distaste. It
grieved them all, but when at last they found, His
Majesty was pleased, their joys were crowned. He
knew, the fairest garden hath some weeds,
He did accept their kind intents, for deeds:
One man there was, that with his zeal too hot,
And furious haste, himself much overshot.
But what man is so foolish, that desires
To get good fruit from thistles, thorns andbriars?
Thus much I thought good to demonstrate here,
Because I saw how much they grieved were;
That any way, the least part of offence,
Should make them seem offensive to their Prince.
Thus three nights was I staid and lodged in *Preston*,

And saw nothing ridiculous to jest on,
Much cost and charge the Mayor upon me spent,
And on my way two miles, with me he went,
There (by good chance) I did more friendship get,
The under Sheriff of *Lancashire* we met,
A gentleman that loved, and knew me well,
And one whose bounteous mind doth bear the bell.
There, as if I had been a noted thief,
The Mayor delivered me unto the Sheriff.
The Sheriff's authority did much prevail,
He sent me unto one that kept the jail.
Thus I perambuling, poor *John Taylor*,
Was given from Mayor to Sheriff, from Sheriff to Jailor.
The Jailor kept an inn, good beds, good cheer,
Where paying nothing, I found nothing dear,
For the under-Sheriff kind Master *Covill* named,
(A man for house-keeping renowed and famed)
Did cause the town of *Lancashire* afford
Me welcome, as if I had been a lord.
And 'tis reported, that for daily bounty,
His mate can scarce be found in all that county.
The extremes of miser, or of prodigal,
He shuns, and lives discreet and liberal,
His wife's mind, and his own are one, so fixed,
That *Argus* eyes could see no odds betwixt,
And sure the difference, (if there difference be)
Is who shall do most good, or he, or she.
Poor folks report, that for relieving them,
He and his wife, are each of them a gem;
At the inn, and at his house two nights I staid,
And what was to be paid, I know he paid:
If nothing of their kindness I had wrote,
Ungrateful me the world might justly note:
Had I declared all I did hear, and see,
For a great flatterer then I deemed should be,
Him and his wife, and modest daughter *Bess*,
With earth, and heaven's felicity, God bless.
Two days a man of his, at his command,
Did guide me to the midst of *Westmoreland*,
And my conductor with a liberal fist,
To keep me moist, scarce any alehouse missed.
The fourth of August (weary, halt, and lame)

17

We in the dark, to a town called *Sedbergh* came,
There Master *Borrowed*, my kind honest host,
Upon me did bestowed unasked cost.
The next day I held on my journey still,
Six miles unto a place called *Carling* hill,
Where Master *Edmund Branthwaite*[10] doth reside,
Who made me welcome, with my man and guide.
Our entertainment, and our fare were such,
It might have satisfied our betters much;
Yet all too little was, his kind heart thought,
And five miles on my way himself me brought,
At *Orton* he, I, and my man did dine,
With Master *Corney* a good true Divine,
And surely Master *Branthwaite*'s well beloved,
His firm integrity is much approved:
His good effects, do make him still affected
Of God and good men, (with regard) respected.
He sent his man with me, o'er dale and down,
Who lodged, and boarded me at *Penrith* town,
And such good cheer, and bedding there I had,
That nothing, (but my weary self) was bad;
There a fresh man, (I know not for whose sake)
With me a journey would to *Carlisle* make:
But from that city, about two miles wide,
Good Sir *John Dalston* lodged me and my guide.
Of all the gentlemen in *England's* bounds
His house is nearest to the Scottish grounds,
And fame proclaims him, far and near, aloud,
He's free from being covetous, or proud;
His son, Sir *George*, most affable, and kind,
His father's image, both in form and mind,
On Saturday to *Carlisle* both did ride,
Where (by their loves and leaves) I did abide,
Where of good entertainment I found store,
From one that was the mayor the year before,
His name is Master *Adam Robinson*,
I the last English friendship with him won.
He (*gratis*) found a guide to bring me through,
  My thanks to Sir John and Sir Geo. Dalston, with Sir Henry Curwin.
From *Carlisle* to the city *Edinburgh*:
This was a help, that was a help alone,
Of all my helps inferior unto none.

Eight miles from *Carlisle* runs a little river,
Which *England's* bounds, from *Scotland's* grounds doth sever.
Without horse, bridge, or boat, I o'er did get
Over Esk I waded. On foot, I went, yet scarce my shoes did wet.
I being come to this long-looked-for land,
Did mark, remark, note, renote, viewed, and scanned;
And I saw nothing that could change my will,
But that I thought myself in *England* still.
The kingdoms are so nearly joined and fixed,
There scarcely went a pair of shears betwixt;
There I saw sky above, and earth below,
And as in *England*, there the sun did show;
The hills with sheep replete, with corn the dale,
The afore-named knights had given money to my guide, of which he left some part at every ale-house.   And many a cottage yielded good Scottish ale;
This county (*Avondale*) in former times,
Was the cursed climate of rebellious crimes:
For *Cumberland* and it, both kingdoms borders,
Were ever ordered, by their own disorders,
Some sharking, shifting, cutting throats, and thieving,
Each taking pleasure in the other's grieving;
And many times he that had wealth to-night,
Was by the morrow morning beggared quite:
Too many years this pell-mell fury lasted,
That all these borders were quite spoiled and wasted,
Confusion, hurly-burly reigned and revelled,
The churches with the lowly ground were levelled;
All memorable monuments defaced,
All places of defence o'erthrown and razed.
That whoso then did in the borders dwell,
Lived little happier than those in hell.
But since the all-disposing God of heaven,
Hath these two kingdoms to one monarch given,
Blest peace, and plenty on them both have showered,
Exile, and hanging hath the thieves devoured,
That now each subject may securely sleep,
His sheep and neat, the black the white doth keep,
For now those crowns are both in one combined,
Those former borders, that each one confine,

Appears to me (as I do understand)
To be almost the centre of the land,
This was a blessed heaven expounded riddle,
To thrust great kingdoms skirts into the middle.
Long may the instrumental cause survive.
From him and his, succession still derive
True heirs unto his virtues, and his throne,
That these two kingdoms ever may be one;
This county of all *Scotland* is most poor,
By reason of the outrages before,
Yet mighty store of corn I saw there grow,
And as good grass as ever man did mow:
And as that day I twenty miles did pass,
I saw eleven hundred neat at grass,
By which may be conjectured at the least,
That there was sustenance for man and beast.
And in the kingdom I have truly scanned,
There's many worser parts, are better manned,
For in the time that thieving was in ure,
The gentles fled to places more secure.
And left the poorer sort, to abide the pain,
Whilst they could ne'er find time to turn again.
The shire of gentlemen is scarce and dainty,
Yet there's relief in great abundance plenty,
Twixt it and England, little odds I see,
They eat, and live, and strong and able be,
So much in verse, and now I'll change my style,
And seriously I'll write in prose awhile.

To the purpose then: my first night's lodging in *Scotland* was at a place called *Moffat*, which they say, is thirty miles from *Carlisle*, but I suppose them to be longer than forty of such miles as are betwixt *London* and Saint *Albans*, (but indeed the Scots do allow almost as large measure of their miles, as they do of their drink, for an English gallon either of ale or wine, is but their quart, and one Scottish mile (now and then, may well stand for a mile and a half or two English) but howsoever short or long, I found that day's journey the weariest that ever I footed; and at night, being come to the town, I found good ordinary country entertainment: my fare and my lodging was sweet and good, and might have served a far better man than myself, although myself have had many times better: but this is to be noted, that though it rained not all the day, yet it was my fortune to be well wet twice, for I waded over a great river called *Esk* in the morning, somewhat more than four miles distance from *Carlisle* in *England*, and at night within two miles of my lodging, I was fain to wade over the river of *Annan* in *Scotland*, from which river the county of *Annandale*, hath its name. And whilst I waded on foot, my man was mounted on horseback, like the *George* without the Dragon. But the next morning, I arose and left *Moffat* behind me, and that day I travelled twenty-one miles to a sorry village called *Blythe*, but I was blithe myself to come to any place of harbour or succour, for since I was born, I never was so weary, or so near being dead with extreme travel: I was foundered and refoundered of all four, and for my better comfort, I came so late, that I must lodge without doors all night, or else in a poor house where the good wife lay in child-bed, her husband being from home, her own servant maid being her nurse. A creature naturally compacted, and artificially adorned with an incomparable homeliness: but as things were I must either take or leave, and necessity made me enter, where we got eggs and ale by measure and by tail. At last to bed I went, my man lying on the floor by me, where in the night there were pigeons did very bountifully mute in his face: the day being no sooner come, and having but fifteen miles to *Edinburgh*, mounted upon my ten toes, and began first to hobble, and after to amble, and so being warm, I fell to pace by degrees; all the way passing through a fertile country for corn and cattle: and about two of the clock in the afternoon that Wednesday, being the thirteenth of August, and the day of *Clare* the Virgin (the sign being in *Virgo*) the moon four days old, the wind at west, I came to take rest, at the wished, long expected, ancient famous city of *Edinburgh*, which I entered like Pierce Penniless,[11] altogether moneyless, but I thank God, not friendless; for being there, for the time of my stay, I might borrow, (if any man would lend) spend if I could get, beg if I had the impudence, and steal, if I durst adventure the price of a hanging, but my purpose was to house my horse, and to suffer him and my apparel to lie in durance, or lavender instead of litter, till such time as I could meet with some valiant friend, that would desperately disburse.

Walking thus down the street, (my body being tired with travel, and my mind attired with moody, muddy, Moor-ditch melancholy) my contemplation did devotely pray, that I might meet one or other to prey upon, being willing to take any slender acquaintance of any map whatsoever, viewing, and circumviewing every man's face I met, as if I meant to draw his picture, but all my acquaintance was *Non est inventus*, (pardon me, reader, that Latin is none of my own, I swear by *Priscian's Pericranium*, an oath which I have ignorantly broken many times.) At last I resolved, that the next gentleman that I meet withal, should be acquaintance whether he would or no: and presently fixing mine eyes upon a gentleman-like object, I looked on him, as if I would survey something through him, and make him my perspective: and he much musing at my gazing, and I much gazing at his musing, at last he crossed the way and made toward me, and then I made down the street from him, leaving to encounter with any man, who came after me leading my horse, whom he thus accosted. My friend (quoth he) doth yonder gentleman, (meaning me) know me, that he looks so wistly on me? Truly sir, said my man, I think not, but my master is a stranger come from *London*, and would gladly meet some acquaintance to direct him where he may have lodging and horse-meat. Presently the gentleman, (being of a generous disposition) overtook me with unexpected and undeserved courtesy, brought me to a lodging, and caused my horse to be put into his own stable, whilst we discoursing over a pint of Spanish, I relate as much English to him, as made him lend me ten shillings, (his name was Master *John Maxwell*) which money I am sure was the first that I handled after I came from out the walls of *London*: but having rested two hours and refreshed myself, the gentleman and I walked to see the City and the Castle, which as my poor unable and unworthy pen can, I will truly describe.

The Castle on a lofty rock is so strongly grounded, bounded, and founded, that by force of man it can never be confounded; the foundation and walls are unpenetrable, the rampiers impregnable, the bulwarks invincible, no way but one it is or can be possible to be made passable. In a word, I have seen many straits and fortresses, in *Germany*, the *Netherlands*, *Spain* and *England*, but they must all give place to this unconquered Castle, both for strength and situation.

Amongst the many memorable things which I was shewed there, I noted especially a great piece of ordnance of iron, it is not for battery, but it will serve to defend a breach, or to toss balls of wild-fire against any that should assail or assault the Castle; it lies now dismounted.[12] And it is so great within, that it was told me that a child was once gotten there: but I, to make trial crept into it, lying on my back, and I am sure there was room enough and spare for a greater than myself.

So leaving the Castle, as it is both defensive against my opposition, and magnific for lodging and receite,[13] I descended lower to the City, wherein I observed the fairest and goodliest street that ever mine eyes beheld, for I did never see or hear of a street of that length, (which is half an English mile from the Castle to a fair port which they call the *Nether-Bow*) and from that port, the street which they call the *Kenny-gate* is one quarter of a mile more, down to the King's Palace, called *Holy-rood-House*, the buildings on each side of the way being all of squared stone, five, six, and seven stories high, and many bye-lanes and closes on each side of the way, wherein are gentlemen's houses, much fairer than the buildings in the High Street, for in the High Street the merchants and tradesmen do dwell, but the gentlemen's mansions and goodliest houses are obscurely founded in the aforesaid lanes: the walls are eight or ten foot thick, exceeding strong, not built for a day, a week, or a month, or a year; but from antiquity to posterity, for many ages; there I found entertainment beyond my expectation or merit, and there is fish, flesh, bread and fruit, in such variety, that I think I may offenceless call it superfluity, or satiety. The worst was, that wine and ale was so scarce, and the people there such misers of it, that every night before I went to bed, if any man had asked me a civil question, all the wit in my head could not have made him a sober answer.

I was at his Majesty's Palace, a stately and princely seat, wherein I saw a sumptuous chapel, most richly adorned with all appurtenances belonging to so sacred a place, or so royal an owner. In the inner court I saw the King's arms cunningly carved in stone, and fixed over a door aloft on the wall, the red lion being in the crest, over which was written this inscription in Latin,

Nobis hæc invicta miserunt, 106 proavi.

I enquired what the English of it was? it was told me as followeth, which I thought worthy to be recorded.

106, forefathers have left this to us unconquered.

This is a worthy and memorable motto, and I think few kingdoms or none in the world can truly write the like, that notwithstanding so many inroads, incursions, attempts, assaults, civil wars, and foreign hostilities, bloody battles, and mighty foughten fields, that maugre the strength and policy of enemies, that royal crown and sceptre hath from one hundred and seven descents, kept still unconquered, and by the power of the King of Kings (through the grace of the Prince of Peace) is now left peacefully to our peaceful king, whom long in blessed peace, the God of peace defend and govern.

But once more, a word or two of *Edinburgh*, although I have scarcely given it that due which belongs unto it, for their lofty and stately buildings, and for their fair and spacious street, yet my mind persuades me that they in former ages that first founded that city did not so well in that they built it in so discommodious a place; for the sea, and all navigable rivers being the chief means for the enriching of towns and cities, by the reason of traffic with foreign nations, with exportation, transportation, and receite of variety of merchandizing; so this city had it been built but one mile lower on the seaside, I doubt not but it had long before this been comparable to many a one of our greatest towns and cities in *Europe*, both for spaciousness of bounds, port, state, and riches. It is said, that King *James* the fifth (of famous memory) did graciously offer to purchase for them, and to bestow upon them freely, certain low and pleasant grounds a mile from them on the seashore, with these conditions, that they should pull down their city, and build it in that more commodious place, but the citizens refused it; and so now it is like (for me), to stand where it doth, for I doubt such another proffer of removal will not be presented to them, till two days after the fair.

Now have with you for *Leith*, whereto I no sooner came, but I was well entertained by Master *Barnard Lindsay*, one of the grooms of his Majesties bed-chamber, he knew my estate was not guilty, because I brought guilt with me (more than my sins, and they would not pass for current there) he therefore did replenish the vaustity[14] of my empty purse, and discharged a piece at me with two bullets of gold, each being in value worth eleven shillings white money; and I was creditably informed, that within the compass of one year, there was shipped away from that only port of *Leith*, fourscore thousand boles of wheat, oats, and barley into *Spain*, *France*, and other foreign parts, and every bole contains the measure of four English bushels, so that from *Leith* only hath been transported three hundred and twenty thousand bushels of corn; besides some hath been shipped away from Saint *Andrews*, from *Dundee*, *Aberdeen*, *Dysart*, *Kirkaldy*, *Kinghorn*, *Burntisland*, *Dunbar*, and other portable towns, which makes me to wonder that a kingdom so populous as it is, should nevertheless sell so much bread-corn beyond the seas, and yet to have more than sufficient for themselves.

So I having viewed the haven and town of *Leith*, took a passage boat to see the new wondrous Well,[15] to which many a one that is not well, comes far and near in hope to be made well: indeed I did hear that it had done much good, and that it hath a rare operation to expel or kill divers maladies; as to provoke appetite, to help much for the avoiding of the gravel in the bladder, to cure sore eyes, and old ulcers, with many other virtues which it hath, but I (through the mercy of God, having no need of it, did make no great inquisition what it had done, but for novelty I drank of it, and I found the taste to be more pleasant than any other water, sweet almost as milk, yet as clear as crystal, and I did observe that though a man did drink a quart, a pottle, or as much as his belly could contain, yet it never offended or lay heavy upon the stomach, no more than if one had drank but a pint or a small quantity.

I went two miles from it to a town called *Burntisland*, where I found many of my especial good friends, as Master *Robert Hay*, one of the Grooms of his Majesty's Bed-chamber, Master *David Drummond*, one of his Gentlemens-

Pensioners, Master *James Acmootye*, one of the Grooms of the Privy Chamber, Captain *Murray*, Sir *Henry Witherington* Knight, Captain *Tyrie*, and divers others: and there Master *Hay*, Master *Drummond*, and the good old Captain *Murray* did very bountifully furnish me with gold for my expenses, but I being at dinner with those aforesaid gentlemen, as we were discoursing, there befel a strange accident, which I think worth the relating.

I know not upon what occasion they began to talk of being at sea in former times, and I (amongst the rest) said, I was at the taking of *Cadiz*; whereto an English gentleman replied, that he was the next good voyage after at the Islands: I answered him that I was there also. He demanded in what ship I was? I told him in the Rainbow of the Queens: why (quoth he) do you not know me? I was in the same ship, and my name is *Witherington*.

Sir, said I, I do remember the name well, but by reason that it is near two and twenty years since I saw you, I may well forget the knowledge of you. Well said he, if you were in that ship, I pray you tell me some remarkable token that happened in the voyage, whereupon I told him two or three tokens; which he did know to be true. Nay then, said I, I will tell you another which (perhaps) you have not forgotten; as our ship and the rest of the fleet did ride at anchor at the Isle of *Flores* (one of the Isles of the *Azores*) there were some fourteen men and boys of our ship, that for novelty would go ashore, and see what fruit the island did bear, and what entertainment it would yield us; so being landed, we went up and down and could find nothing but stones, heath and moss, and we expected oranges, lemons, figs, muskmellions, and potatoes; in the mean space the wind did blow so stiff, and the sea was so extreme rough, that our ship-boat could not come to the land to fetch us, for fear she should be beaten in pieces against the rocks; this continued five days, so that we were almost famished for want of food: but at last (I squandering up and down) by the providence of God I happened into a cave or poor habitation, where I found fifteen loaves of bread, each of the quantity of a penny loaf in *England*, I having a valiant stomach of the age of almost of a hundred and twenty hours breeding, fell to, and ate two loaves and never said grace: and as I was about to make a horse-loaf of the third loaf, I did put twelve of them into my breeches, and my sleeves, and so went mumbling out of the cave, leaning my back against a tree, when upon the sudden a gentleman came to me, and said, "Friend, what are you eating?" "Bread," (quoth I,) "For God's sake," said he, "give me some." With that, I put my hand into my breech, (being my best pantry) and I gave him a loaf, which he received with many thanks, and said, that if ever he could requit it, he would.

I had no sooner told this tale, but Sir *Henry Witherington* did acknowledge himself to be the man that I had given the loaf unto two and twenty years before, where I found the proverb true, that men have more privilege than mountains in meeting.

In what great measure he did requite so small a courtesy, I will relate in this following discourse in my return through *Northumberland*: so leaving my man at the town of *Burntisland*, I told him, I would but go to *Stirling*, and see the Castle there, and withal to see my honourable friends the Earl of *Mar*, and Sir *William Murray* Knight, Lord of *Abercairney*, and that I would return within two days at the most: but it fell out quite contrary; for it was and five and thirty days before I could get back again out of these noble men's company. The whole progress of my travel with them, and the cause of my stay I cannot with gratefulness omit; and thus it was.

A worthy gentleman named Master *John Fenton*, did bring me on my way six miles to *Dunfermline*, where I was well entertained, and lodged at Master *John Gibb* his house, one of the Grooms of his Majesty's Bed-chamber, and I think the oldest servant the King hath: withal, I was well entertained there by Master *Crighton* at his own house, who went with me, and shewed me the Queens Palace; (a delicate and Princely Mansion) withal I saw the ruins of an ancient and stately built Abbey, with fair gardens, orchards, meadows belonging to the Palace: all which with fair and goodly revenues by the suppression of the Abbey, were annexed to the crown. There also I saw a very fair church, which though it be now very large and spacious, yet it hath in former times been much larger. But I taking my leave of *Dunfermline*, would needs go and see the truly noble Knight Sir *George Bruce*, at a town called the *Culross*: there he made me right welcome, both with variety of fare, and after all, he commanded three of his men to direct me to see his most admirable coal mines; which (if man can or could work wonders) is a wonder; for myself neither in any travels that I have been in, nor any history that I have read, or any discourse that I have heard, did never see, read, or hear of any work of man that might parallel or be equivalent with this unfellowed and unmatchable work: and though all I can say of it, cannot describe it according to the worthiness of his vigilant industry, that was both the occasion, inventor, and maintainer of it: yet rather than the memory of so rare an enterprise, and so accomplished a profit to the commonwealth shall be raked and smothered in the dust of oblivion, I will give a little touch at the description of it, although I amongst writers, am like he that worse may hold the candle.

The mine hath two ways into it, the one by sea and the other by land; but a man may go into it by land, and return the same way if he please, and so he may enter into it by sea, and by sea he may come forth of it: but I for variety's sake went in by sea, and out by land. Now men may object, how can a man go into a mine, the entrance of it being into the sea, but that the sea will follow him, and so drown the mine? To which objection thus I answer, that at low water mark, the sea being ebbed away, and a great part of the sand bare; upon this

same sand (being mixed with rocks and crags) did the master of this great work build a round circular frame of stone, very thick, strong, and joined together with glutinous or bituminous matter, so high withal that the sea at the highest flood, or the greatest rage of storm or tempest, can neither dissolve the stones so well compacted in the building or yet overflow the height of it. Within this round frame, (at all adventures) he did set workmen to dig with mattocks, pickaxes, and other instruments fit for such purposes. They did dig forty feet down right into and through a rock. At last they found that which they expected, which was sea coal, they following the vein of the mine, did dig forward still: so that in the space of eight and twenty, or nine and twenty years, they have digged more than an English mile under the sea, so that when men are at work below, an hundred of the greatest ships in *Britain* man sail over their heads. Besides, the mine is most artificially cut like an arch or a vault, all that great length, with many nooks and bye-ways: and it is so made, that a man may walk upright in the most places, both in and out. Many poor people are there set on work, which otherwise through the want of employment would perish. But when I had seen the mine, and was come forth of it again; after my thanks given to Sir *George Bruce*, I told him, that if the plotters of the

Powder Treason in England had seen this mine, that they (perhaps) would have attempted to have left the Parliament House, and have undermined the Thames, and so to have blown up the barges and wherries, wherein the King, and all the estates of our kingdom were. Moreover, I said, that I couldafford to turn tapster at *London*, so that I had but
one quarter of a mile of his mine to make me
a cellar, to keep beer and bottled ale
in. But leaving these jests in
prose, I will relate a few
verses that I made
merrily of this
mine.

that have wasted, months, weeks, days, and hours
In viewing kingdoms, countries, towns, and towers,
Without all measure, measuring many paces,
And with my pen describing many places,
With few additions of mine own devising,
(Because I have a smack of *Coryatizing*[16])
Our *Mandeville*, *Primaleon*, *Don Quixote*,
Great *Amadis*, or *Huon*, travelled not
As I have done, or been where I have been,
Or heard and seen, what I have heard and seen;
Nor Britain's *Odcombe* (*Zany* brave *Ulysses*)
In all his ambling, saw the like as this is.
I was in (would I could describe it well)
A dark, light, pleasant, profitable hell,
And as by water I was wafted in,
I thought that I in *Charon's* boat had been,
But being at the entrance landed thus,
Three men there (instead of *Cerberus*)
Convey'd me in, in each one hand a light
To guide us in that vault of endless night,
There young and old with glim'ring candles burning
Dig, delve, and labour, turning and returning,
Some in a hole with baskets and with bags,
Resembling furies, or infernal hags:
There one like *Tantalus* feeding, and there one,
Like *Sisyphus* he rolls the restless stone.
Yet all I saw was pleasure mixed with profit,
Which proved it to be no tormenting Tophet[17]
For in this honest, worthy, harmless hell,
There ne'er did any damned Devil dwell;
And th' owner of it gains by 't more true glory,
Than *Rome* doth by fantastic Purgatory.
A long mile thus I passed, down, down, steep, steep,
In deepness far more deep, than *Neptunes* deep,
Whilst o'er my head (in fourfold stories high)
Was earth, and sea, and air, and sun, and sky:
That had I died in that *Cimmerian*[18] room,
Four elements had covered o'er my tomb:
Thus farther than the bottom did I go,
(And many Englishmen have not done so;)
Where mounting porpoises, and mountain whales,

And regiments of fish with fins and scales,
'Twixt me and heaven did freely glide and slide,
And where great ships may at an anchor ride:
Thus in by sea, and out by land I past,
And took my leave of good Sir *George* at last.

The sea at certain places doth leak, or soak into the mine, which by the industry of Sir *George Bruce*, is all conveyed to one well near the land; where he hath a device like a horse-mill, that with three horses and a great chain of iron, going downward many fathoms, with thirty-six buckets fastened to the chain, of the which eighteen go down still to be filled, and eighteen ascend up to be emptied, which do empty themselves (without any man's labour) into a trough that conveys the water into the sea again; by which means he saves his mine, which otherwise would be destroyed with the sea, besides he doth make every week ninety or a hundred tons of salt, which doth serve most part of *Scotland*, some he sends into *England*, and very much into *Germany*: all which shows the painful industry with God's blessings to such worthy endeavours: I must with many thanks remember his courtesy to me, and lastly how he sent his man to guide me ten miles on the way to *Stirling*, where by the way I saw the outside of a fair and stately house called *Allaway*, belonging to the Earl of *Mar* which by reason that his honour was not there, I past by and went to *Stirling*, where I was entertained and lodged at one Master John *Archibalds*, where all my want was that I wanted room to contain half the good cheer that I might have had there! he had me into the castle, which in few words I do compare to *Windsor* for situation, much more than *Windsor* in strength, and somewhat less in greatness: yet I dare affirm that his Majesty hath not such another hall to any house that he hath neither in *England* or *Scotland*, except Westminster Hall which is now no dwelling hall for a prince, being long since metamorphosed into a house for the law and the profits.

This goodly hall was built by King *James* the fourth, that married King *Henry* the Eight's sister, and after was slain at *Flodden field*; but it surpasses all the halls for dwelling houses that ever I saw, for length, breadth, height and strength of building, the castle is built upon a rock very lofty, and much beyond *Edinburgh* Castle in state and magnificence, and not much inferior to it in strength, the rooms of it are lofty, with carved works on the ceilings, the doors of each room being so high, that a man may ride upright on horseback into any chamber or lodging. There is also a goodly fair chapel, with cellars, stables, and all other necessary offices, all very stately and befitting the majesty of a king.

From *Stirling* I rode to Saint *Johnstone*,[19] a fine town it is, but it is much decayed, by reason of the want of his Majesty's yearly coming to lodge there.

There I lodged one night at an inn, the goodman of the house his name being *Patrick Pitcairne*, where my entertainment was with good cheer, good lodging, all too good to a bad weary guest. Mine host told me that the Earl of *Mar*, and Sir *William Murray* of *Abercairney* were gone to the great hunting to the *Brae* of *Mar*[20]; but if I made haste I might perhaps find them at a town called *Brekin*, or *Brechin*, two and thirty miles from Saint *Johnstone* whereupon I took a guide to *Brechin* the next day, but before I came, my lord was gone from thence four days.

Then I took another guide, which brought me such strange ways over mountains and rocks, that I think my horse never went the like; and I am sure I never saw any ways that might fellow them I did go through a country called *Glen Esk*, where passing by the side of a hill, so steep as the ridge of a house, where the way was rocky, and not above a yard broad in some places, so fearful and horrid it was to look down into the bottom, for if either horse or man had slipped, he had fallen without recovery a good mile downright; but I thank God, at night I came to a lodging in the Laird of *Edzell's* land, where I lay at an Irish house, the folks not being able to speak scarce any English, but I supped and went to bed, where I had not laid long, but I was enforced to rise, I was so stung with Irish mosquitoes, a creature that hath six legs, and lives like a monster altogether upon man's flesh, they do inhabit and breed most in sluttish houses, and this house was none of the cleanest, the beast is much like a louse in *England*, both in shape and nature; in a word, they were to me the *A.* and the *Z.* the prologue and the epilogue, the first and the last that I had in all my travels from *Edinburgh*; and had not this Highland Irish house helped me at a pinch, I should have sworn that all *Scotland* had not been so kind as to have bestowed a louse upon me: but with a shift that I had, I shifted off my cannibals, and was never more troubled with them.

The next day I travelled over an exceeding high mountain, called mount *Skene*, where I found the valley very warm before I went up it; but when I came to the top of it, my teeth began to dance in my head with cold, like Virginal's jacks;[21] and withal, a most familiar mist embraced me round, that I could not see thrice my length any way: withal, it yielded so friendly a dew, that did moisten through all my clothes: where the old Proverb of a Scottish mist was verified, in wetting me to the skin. Up and down, I think this hill is six miles, the way so uneven, stony, and full of bogs, quagmires, and long heath, that a dog with three legs will out-run a horse with four; for do what we could, we were four hours before we could pass it.

Thus with extreme travel, ascending and descending, mounting and alighting, I came at night to the place where I would be, in the Brae of *Mar*, which is a large county, all composed of such mountains, that Shooter's Hill,

Gad's Hill, Highgate Hill, Hampstead Hill, Birdlip Hill, or Malvern's Hills, are but mole-hills in comparison, or like a liver, or a gizard under a capon's wing, in respect of the altitude of their tops, or perpendicularity of their bottoms. There I saw Mount *Ben Aven*, with a furred mist upon his snowy head instead of a night-cap: (for you must understand, that the oldest man alive never saw but the snow was on the top of divers of those hills, both in summer, as well as in winter.) There did I find the truly Noble and Right Honourable Lords *John Erskine* Earl of Mar, *James Stuart* Earl of Murray, *George Gordon* Earl of Enzie, son and heir to the Marquess of Huntly, *James Erskine* Earl of Buchan, and *John* Lord *Erskine*, son and heir to the Earl of Mar, and their Countesses, with my much honoured, and my best assured and approved friend, Sir *William Murray* Knight, of *Abercairney*, and hundred of others Knights, Esquires, and their followers; all and every man in general in one habit, as if *Lycurgus* had been there, and made laws of equality: for once in the year, which is the whole month of August, and sometimes part of September, many of the nobility and gentry of the kingdom (for their pleasure) do come into these Highland Countries to hunt, where they do conform themselves to the habit of the Highland men, who for the most part speak nothing but Irish; and in former time were those people which were called the *Red-shanks*.[22] Their habit is shoes with but one sole apiece; stockings (which they call short hose) made of a warm stuff of diverscolours, which they call tartan: as for breeches, many of them, nor their forefathers never wore any, but a jerkin of the same stuff that their hose is of, their garters being bands or wreaths of hay or straw, with a plaid about their shoulders, which is a mantle of divers colours, of much finer and lighter stuff than their hose, with blue flat caps on their heads, a handkerchief knit with two knots about their neck; and thus are they attired. Now their weapons are long bows and forked arrows, swords and targets, harquebusses, muskets, dirks, and Lochaber axes. With these arms I found many of them armed for the hunting. As for their attire, any man of what degree soever that comes amongst them, must not disdain to wear it; for if they do, then they will disdain to hunt, or willingly, to bring in their dogs: but if men be kind unto them, and be in their habit; then are they conquered with kindness, and the sport will be plentiful. This was the reason that I found so many noblemen and gentlemen in those shapes. But to proceed to the hunting.

My good Lord of *Mar* having put me into that shape,[23] I rode with him from his house, where I saw the ruins of an old castle, called the castle of *Kindroghit* [Castletown]. It was built by King *Malcolm Canmore* (for a hunting house) who reigned in *Scotland* when *Edward* the Confessor, *Harold*, and Norman *William* reigned in *England*: I speak of it, because it was the last house that I saw in those parts; for I was the space of twelve days after, before I saw either house, corn field, or habitation for any creature, but deer, wild horses, wolves, and such like creatures, which made me doubt that I should never have seen a house again.[24]

Thus the first day we travelled eight miles, where there small cottages built on purpose to lodge in, which they call Lonchards, I thank my good Lord *Erskine*, he commanded that I should always be lodged in his lodging, the kitchen being always on the side of a bank, many kettles and pots boiling, and many spits turning and winding, with great variety of cheer: as venison baked, sodden, roast, and stewed beef, mutton, goats, kid, hares, fresh salmon, pigeons, hens, capons, chickens, partridge, moor-coots, heath-cocks, capercailzies, and termagants [ptarmigans]; good ale, sack, white, and claret, tent, (or Alicante) with most potent *Aquavitæ*.

All these, and more than these we had continually, in superfluous abundance, caught by Falconers, Fowlers, Fishers, and brought by my Lord's tenants and purveyors to victual our camp, which consisted of fourteen or fifteen hundred men and horses; the manner of the hunting is this: five or six hundred men do rise early in the morning, and they do disperse themselves divers ways, and seven, eight, or ten miles compass, they do bring or chase in the deer in many herds, (two, three, or four hundred in a herd) to such or such a place, as the Nobleman shall appoint them; then when day is come, the Lords and gentlemen of their companies, do ride or go to the said places, sometimes wading up to their middles through bournes and rivers: and then: they being come to the place, do lie down on the ground, till those foresaid scouts which are called the Tinchel, do bring down the deer: but as the proverb says of a bad cook, so these Tinchel-men do lick their own fingers; for besides their bows and arrows, which they carry with them, we can hear now and then a harquebuss or a musket go off, which they do seldom discharge in vain: Then after we had stayed there three hours or thereabouts, we might perceive the deer appear on the hills round about us, (their heads making a show like a wood) which being followed close by the Tinchel, are chased down into the valley where we lay; then all the valley on each side being waylaid with a hundred couple of strong Irish greyhounds, they are let loose as the occasion serves upon the herd of deer, so that with dogs, guns, arrows, dirks, and daggers, in the space of two hours, fourscore fat deer were slain, which after are disposed of some one way, and some another, twenty and thirty miles, and more than enough left for us to make merry withal at our rendezvous. I liked the sport so well, that I made these two sonnets following.

hy should I waste invention to indite,
Ovidian fictions, or Olympian games?
My misty Muse enlightened with more light,
To a more noble pitch her aim she frames.
I must relate to my great Master JAMES,
The Caledonian annual peaceful war;
How noble minds do eternize their fames,
By martial meeting in the Brae of *Mar*:
How thousand gallant spirits came near and far,
With swords and targets, arrows, bows, and guns,
That all the troop to men of judgment, are
The God of Wars great never conquered sons,
The sport is manly, yet none bleed but beasts,
And last the victor on the vanquished feasts.

f sport like this can on the mountains be,
Where *Phœbus* flames can never melt the snow;
Then let who list delight in vales below,
Sky-kissing mountains pleasure are for me:
What braver object can man's eyesight see,
Than noble, worshipful, and worthy wights,
As if they were prepared for sundry fights,
Yet all in sweet society agree?
Through heather, moss, 'mongst frogs, and bogs, and fogs,
'Mongst craggy cliffs, and thunder-battered hills,
Hares, hinds, bucks, roes, are chased by men and dogs,
Where two hours hunting fourscore fat deer kills.
Lowland, your sports are low as is your seat,

The Highland games and minds, are high and great.

Being come to our lodgings, there was such baking, boiling, roasting, and stewing, as if Cook Ruffian had been there to have scalded the devil in his feathers: and after supper a fire of fir-wood as high as an indifferent May- pole: for I assure you, that the Earl of *Mar* will give any man that is his friend, for thanks, as many fir trees (that are as good as any ship's masts in England) as are worth if they were in any place near the Thames, or any other portable river) the best earldom in England or Scotland either: For I dare affirm, he hath as many growing there, as would serve for masts (from this time to the end of the world) for all the ships, caracks, hoys, galleys, boats, drumlers, barks, and water-crafts, that are now, or can be in the world these forty years.

This sounds like a lie to an unbeliever; but I and many thousands do know that I speak within the compass of truth: for indeed (the more is the pity) they do grow so far from any passage of water, and withal in such rocky mountains, that no way to convey them is possible to be passable, either with boat, horse, or cart.

Thus having spent certain days in hunting in the Brae of *Mar*, we went to the next county called *Badenoch*, belonging to the Earl of *Enzie*, where having such sport and entertainment as we formerly had; after four or five days pastime, we took leave of hunting for that year; and took our journey toward a strong house of the Earl's, called *Ruthven* in *Badenoch*, where my Lord of *Enzie* and his noble Countess (being daughter to the Earl of *Argyle*) did give us most noble welcome three days.

From thence we went to a place called *Balloch Castle*,[25] a fair and stately house, a worthy gentleman being the owner of it, called the Laird of *Grant*; his wife being a gentlewoman honourably descended being sister to the right Honourable Earl of *Athol*, and to Sir *Patrick Murray* Knight; she being both inwardly and outwardly plentifully adorned with the gifts of grace and nature: so that our cheer was more than sufficient; and yet much less than they could afford us. There stayed there four days, four Earls, one Lord, divers Knights and Gentlemen, and their servants, footmen and horses; and every meal four long tables furnished with all varieties: our first and second course being three score dishes at one board; and after that always a banquet: and there if I had not forsworn wine till I came to *Edinburgh* I think I had there drunk my last.

The fifth day with much ado we gate from thence to *Tarnaway*, a goodly house of the Earl of *Murrays*,[26] where that Right Honourable Lord and his Lady did welcome us four days more. There was good cheer in all variety, with somewhat more than plenty for advantage: for indeed the County of

Murray is the most pleasantest and plentiful country in all *Scotland*; being plain land, that a coach may be driven more than four and thirty miles one way in it, alongst by the sea-coast.

From thence I went to *Elgin* in *Murray*,[27] an ancient City, where there stood a fair and beautiful church with three steeples, the walls of it and the steeples all yet standing; but the roofs, windows, and many marble monuments and tombs of honourable and worthy personages all broken and defaced: this was done in the time when ruin bare rule, and Knox knocked down churches.

From *Elgin* we went to the Bishop of *Murray* his house which is called *Spiny*, or *Spinay*: a Reverend Gentleman he is, of the noble name of *Douglas*, where we were very well welcomed, as befitted the honour of himself and his guests.

From thence we departed to the Lord Marquess of *Huntlys* to a sumptuous house of his, named the *Bog of Geethe*, where our entertainment was like himself, free, bountiful and honourable. There (after two days stay) with much entreaty and earnest suit, I gate leave of the Lords to depart towards *Edinburgh*: the Noble Marquess, the Earl of *Mar*, *Murray*, *Enzie*, *Buchan*, and the Lord *Erskine*; all these, I thank them, gave me gold to defray my charges in my journey.

So after five and thirty days hunting and travel I returning, past by another stately mansion of the Lord Marquesses, called *Stroboggy*, and so over *Carny* mount to *Brechin*, where a wench that was born deaf and dumb came into my chamber at midnight (I being asleep) and she opening the bed, would feign have lodged with me: but had I been a *Sardanapalus*, or a *Heliogabulus*, I think that either the great travel over the mountains had tamed me; or if not, her beauty could never have moved me. The best parts of her were, that her breath was as sweet as sugar-candian,[28] being very well shouldered beneath the waste; and as my hostess told me the next morning, that she had changed her maiden-head for the price of a bastard not long before. But howsoever, she made such a hideous noise, that I started out of my sleep, and thought that the Devil had been there: but I no sooner knew who it was, but I arose, and thrust my dumb beast out of my chamber; and for want of a lock or a latch, I staked up my door with a great chair.

Thus having escaped one of the seven deadly sins as at *Brechin*, I departed from thence to a town called *Forfor*; and from thence to *Dundee*, and so to *Kinghorn*, *Burntisland*, and so to *Edinburgh*, where I stayed eight days, to recover myself of falls and bruises, which I received in my travel in the Highland mountainous hunting. Great welcome I had showed me all my stay at *Edinburgh*, by many worthy gentlemen, namely, old Master *George Todrigg*, Master *Henry Livingston*, Master *James Henderson*, Master *John Maxwell*, and a number of others, who suffered me to want no wine or good cheer, as may be imagined.

Now the day before I came from *Edinburgh*, I went to *Leith*, where I found my long approved and assured good friend Master *Benjamin Jonson*, at one Master *John Stuarts* house; I thank him for his great kindness towards me: for at my taking leave of him, he gave me a piece of gold of two and twenty shillings[29] to drink his health in *England*. And withal, willed me to remember his kind commendations to all his friends: So with a friendly farewell, I left him as well, as I hope never to see him in a worse estate: for he is amongst noblemen and gentlemen that know his true worth, and their own honours, where, with much respective love he is worthily entertained.

So leaving *Leith* I returned to *Edinburgh*, and within the port or gate, called the *Nether-Bow*, I discharged my pockets of all the money I had: and as I came pennyless within the walls of that city at my first coming thither; so now at my departing from thence, I came moneyless out of it again; having in company to convey me out, certain gentlemen, amongst the which Master *James Acherson*, Laird of *Gasford*, a gentleman that brought me to his house, where with great entertainment he and his good wife did welcome me.

On the morrow he sent one of his men to bring me to a place called *Adam*, to Master *John Acmootye* his house, one of the Grooms of his Majesty's Bed-chamber; where with him and his two brethren, Master *Alexander*, and Master *James Acmootye*, I found both cheer and welcome, not inferior to any that I had had in any former place.

Amongst our viands that we had there, I must not forget the Sole and Goose (*sic*), a most delicate fowl, which breeds in great abundance in a little rock called the *Bass*, which stands two miles into the sea. It is very good flesh, but it is eaten in the form as we eat oysters, standing at a side-board, a little before dinner, unsanctified without grace; and after it is eaten, it must be well liquored with two or three good rouses[30] of sherry or canary sack. The Lord or owner of the *Bass* doth profit at the least two hundred pound yearly by those geese; the *Bass* itself being of a great height, and near three quarters of a mile in compass, all fully replenished with wild fowl, having but one small entrance into it, with a house, a garden, and a chapel in it; and on the top of it a well of pure fresh water.

From *Adam*, Master *John* and Master *James Acmootye* went to the town of *Dunbar* with me, where ten Scottish pints of wine were consumed, and brought to nothing for a farewell: there at Master *James Baylies* house I took leave, and Master *James Acmootye* coming for *England*, said, that if I would ride with, that neither I nor my horse should want betwixt that place and *London*. Now I having no money nor means for travel, began at once to examine my manners and my want: at last my want persuaded my manners to accept of this worthy gentleman's undeserved courtesy. So that night he brought me to a place called *Cockburnspath*, where we lodged at an inn, the like of which I dare say, is not in any of his Majesty's Dominions. And for to show my thankfulness to Master *William Arnot* and his wife, the owners thereof, I must explain their bountiful entertainment of guests, which is this:

Suppose ten, fifteen, or twenty men and horses come to lodge at their house, the men shall have flesh, tame and wild fowl, fish with all variety of good cheer, good lodging, and welcome; and the horses shall want neither hay or provender: and at the morning at their departure the reckoning is just nothing. This is this worthy gentlemen's use, his chief delight being only to give strangers entertainment *gratis*: and I am sure, that in *Scotland* beyond *Edinburgh*, I have been at houses like castles for building; the master of the house his beaver being his blue bonnet, one that will wear no other shirts, but of the flax that grows on his own ground, and of his wife's, daughters', or servants' spinning; that hath his stockings, hose, and jerkin of the wool of his own sheep's backs; that never (by his pride of apparel) caused mercer, draper, silk-man, embroiderer, or haberdasher to break and turn bankrupt: and yet this plain home-spun fellow keeps and maintains thirty, forty, fifty servants, or perhaps, more, every day relieving three or fourscore poor people at his gate; and besides all this, can give noble entertainment for four or five days together to five or six earls and lords, besides knights, gentlemen and their followers, if they be three or four hundred men, and horse of them, where they shall not only feed but feast, and not feast but banquet, this is a man that desires to know nothing so much, as his duty to God and his King, whose greatest cares are to practise the works of piety, charity, and hospitality: he never studies the consuming art of fashionless fashions, he never tries his strength to bear four or five hundred acres on his back at once, his legs are always at liberty, not being fettered with golden garters, and manacled with artificial roses, whose weight (sometime) is the last reliques of some decayed Lordship: Many of these worthy housekeepers there are in *Scotland*, amongst some of them I was entertained; from whence I did truly gather these aforesaid observations.

So leaving *Cockburnspath*, we rode to *Berwick*, where the worthy old Soldier and ancient Knight, Sir *William Bowyer*, made me welcome, but contrary to his will, we lodged at an Inn, where Master *James Acmootye* paid all charges: but at *Berwick* there was a grievous chance happened, which I think not fit the relation to be omitted.

In the river of *Tweed*, which runs by *Berwick*, are taken by fishermen that dwell there, infinite numbers of fresh salmons, so that many households and families are relieved by the profit of that fishing; but (how long since I know not) there was an order that no man or boy whatsoever should fish upon a Sunday: this order continued long amongst them, till some eight or nine weeks before Michaelmas last, on a Sunday, the salmons played in such great abundance in the river, that some of the fishermen (contrary to God's law and their own order) took boats and nets and fished, and caught near three hundred salmons; but from that time until Michaelmas day that I was there, which was nine weeks, and heard the report of it, and saw the poor people's miserable lamentations, they had not seen one salmon in the river; and some of them were in despair that they should never see any more there; affirming it to be God's judgment upon them for the profanation of the Sabbath.

The thirtieth of September we rode from *Berwick* to *Belford* from *Belford* to *Alnwick*, the next day from *Alnwick* to *Newcastle*, where I found the noble Knight, Sir *Henry Witherington*; who, because I would have no gold nor silver, gave me a bay mare, in requital of a loaf of bread that I had given him two and twenty years before, at the Island of *Flores*, of the which I have spoken before. I overtook at *Newcastle* a great many of my worthy friends, which were all coming for *London*, namely, Master *Robert Hay*, and Master *David Drummond*, where I was welcomed at Master *Nicholas Tempests* house. From *Newcastle* I rode with those gentlemen to *Durham*, to *Darlington*, to *Northallerton*, and to *Topcliffe* in *Yorkshire*, where I took my leave of them, and would needs try my pennyless fortunes by myself, and see the city of *York*, where I was lodged at my right worshipful good friend, Master Doctor *Hudson* one of his Majesty's chaplains, who went with me, and shewed me the goodly Minster Church there, and the most admirable, rare-wrought, unfellowed[31] chapter house.

From *York* I rode to *Doncaster*, where my horses were well fed at the Bear, but myself found out the honorable Knight, Sir *Robert Anstruther* at his father-in-law's, the truly noble Sir *Robert Swifts* house, he being then High Sheriff of *Yorkshire*, where with their good Ladies, and the right Honourable the Lord *Sanquhar*, I was stayed two nights and one day, Sir *Robert Anstruther* (I thank him) not only paying for my two horses' meat, but at my departure, he gave me a letter to *Newark* upon *Trent*, twenty eight miles in my way, where Master *George Atkinson* mine host made me as welcome, as if I had been a French Lord, and what was to be paid, as I called for nothing, I paid as much; and left the reckoning with many thanks to Sir *Robert Anstruther*.

So leaving *Newark*, with another gentleman that overtook me, we came at night to *Stamford*, to the sign of the Virginity (or the Maidenhead) where I delivered a letter from the Lord *Sanquhar*; which caused Master *Bates* and his wife, being the master and mistress of the house, to make me and the gentleman that was with me great cheer for nothing.

From *Stamford* the next day we rode to *Huntington*, where we lodged at the Postmaster's house, at the sign of the Crown; his name is *Riggs*. He was informed who I was, and wherefore I undertook this my pennyless progress: wherefore he came up to our chamber, and supped with us, and very bountifully called for three quarts of wine and sugar, and four jugs of beer. He did drink and begin healths like a horse-leech and swallowed down his cups without feeling, as if he had had the dropsy, or nine pound of sponge in his maw. In a word, as he is a post, he drank post, striving and calling by all means to make the reckoning great, or to make us men of great reckoning. But in his payment he was tired like a jade, leaving the gentleman that was with me to discharge the terrible shot, or else one of my horses must have lain in pawn for his superfluous calling, and unmannerly intrusion.

But leaving him, I left *Huntington*, and rode on the Sunday to *Puckeridge*, where Master *Holland* at the Falcon, (mine old acquaintance) and my loving and ancient host gave me, my friend, my man, and our horses excellent cheer, and welcome, and I paid him with, not a penny of money.

The next day I came to *London*, and obscurely coming within Moorgate, I went to a house and borrowed money: and so I stole back again to *Islington*, to the sign of the Maidenhead,[32] staying till Wednesday, that my friends came to meet me, who knew no other, but that Wednesday was my first coming; where with all love I was entertained with much good cheer: and after supper we had a play of the Life and Death of *Guy of Warwick*,[33] played by the Right Honourable the Earl of *Derby* his men. And so on the Thursday morning being the fifteenth of October, I came home to my house in *London*.

THE EPILOGUE TO ALL MY ADVENTURERS
AND OTHERS.

hus did I neither spend, or beg, or ask,
By any course, direct or indirectly:
But in each tittle I performed my task,
According to my bill most circumspectly.
I vow to God, I have done SCOTLAND wrong,
(And (justly) against me it may bring an action)
I have not given it that right which doth belong,
For which I am half guilty of detraction:
Yet had I wrote all things that there I saw,
Misjudging censures would suppose I flatter,
And so my name I should in question draw,
Where asses bray, and prattling pies do chatter:
Yet (armed with truth) I publish with my pen,
That there the Almighty doth his blessings heap,
In such abundant food for beasts and men;
That I ne'er saw more plenty or more cheap.
Thus what mine eyes did see, I do believe;
And what I do believe, I know is true:
And what is true unto your hands I give,
That what I give, may be believed of you.
But as for him that says I lie or dote,
I do return, and turn the lie in's throat.
   Thus gentlemen, amongst you take my ware,
   You share my thanks, and I your moneys share.

Yours in all observance and gratefulness,
ever to be commanded,

JOHN TAYLOR.

FINIS.

[1] PROVANT.—Provender; provision.

[2] FEGARY.—A vagary.

[3] TRUNDLE.—*i.e.*, John Trundle of the sign of *No-body* (see note page 6).

[4] It is reasonable to conjecture that at this date the custom of "Swearing-in at Highgate was not in vogue—or, *No-body* would have taken the oath.

[5] NAMED LEAN AND FEN.—Some jest is intended here on the Host's name.—Qy., Leanfen, or, the anagram of A. FENNEL.

[6] NO-BODY was the singular sign of John Trundle, a ballad-printer in Barbican in the seventeenth century [and who seems to have accompanied our author as far as *Whetstone* on his "Penniless Pilgrimage"—and, certainly up to this point a very "wet" one!] In one of Ben Jonson's plays Nobody is introduced, "attyred in a payre of Breeches, which were made to come up to his neck, with his armes out at his pockets and cap drowning his face." This comedy was "printed for John Trundle and are to be sold at his shop in Barbican at the sygne of No-Body." A unique ballad, preserved in the Miller Collection at Britwell House, entitled "The Well-spoken No-body," is accompanied by a woodcut representing a ragged barefooted fool on pattens, with a torn money-bag under his arm, walking through a chaos of broken pots, pans, bellows, candlesticks, tongs, tools, windows, &c. Above him is a scroll in black-letter:—

"Nobody.is.my.Name.that.Beyreth.Every.Bodyes.Blame."

The ballad commences as follows:—

"Many speke of Robin Hoode that never shott in his bowe,
So many have layed faultes to me, which I did never knowe;
　　　But nowe, beholde, here I am,
　　　Whom all the worlde doeth diffame;
　　　Long have they also scorned me,
　　　And locked my mouthe for speking free.
　　　As many a Godly man they have so served
　　　Which unto them God's truth hath shewed;
　　　Of such they have burned and hanged some.
　　　That unto their ydolatrye wold not come:
　　　The Ladye Truthe they have locked in cage,
　　　Saying of her Nobodye had knowledge.
　　　For as much nowe as they name Nobodye
　　　I thinke verilye they speke of me:
　　　Whereffore to answere I nowe beginne—
　　　The locke of my mouthe is opened with ginne,

> Wrought by no man, but by God's grace,
> Unto whom be prayse in every place," &c.

Larwood and Hotten's *History of Signboards*.

[7] PULSE.—All sorts of leguminous seeds.

[8] See Dedication to *The Scourge of Baseness*.

[9] MASTER DOCTOR HOLLAND.—The once well-known Philemon Holland, Physician, and "Translator-General of his Age," published translations of Livy, 1600; Pliny's "Natural History," 1601; Camden's "Britannica," &c. He is said to have used in translation more paper and fewer pens than any other writer before or since, and who "would not let Suetonius be Tranquillus." Born at Chelmsford, 1551; died 1636.

[10] EDMUND BRANTHWAITE.—Robert Branthwaite, William Branthwaite *Cant.*, and "Thy assured friend" R. B., have each written Commendatory Verses to ALL THE WORKS OF JOHN TAYLOR. London 1630. And Southey in his "Lives and Works of Uneducated Poets," has the following:—"One might have hoped in these parts for a happy meeting between John Taylor and Barnabee, of immortal memory; indeed it is likely that the Water-Poet and the Anti-Water-Poet were acquainted, and that the latter may have introduced him to his connections hereabout, Branthwaite being the same name as Brathwait, and Barnabee's brother having married a daughter of this Sir John Dalston."

[11] PIERCE PENNILESS, by Thomas Nash. London, 1592.

[12] This "ordnance of iron" still exists there, and is historically known as "Mons Meg" and popularly as "Long Meg."

[13] RECEITE.—A receptacle.

[14] VAUSTITY.—Emptiness.

[15] *See* Anderson's The Cold Spring of Kinghorn Craig, Edinb. 1618.

[16] CORYATIZING.—Thomas Coryate, an English traveller, who called himself the "Odcombian leg-stretcher." He was the son of the rector of Odcombe, and in 1611 published an account of his travels on the Continent with the singular title of "Coryates Crudities. Hastily gobled up in five Moneths travells in France, Savoy, Italy, Rhetia, commonly called the Grisons country, Helvetia, alias Switzerland, some parts of high Germany, and the Netherlands; Newly digested in the hungary aire of Odcombe in the county of Somerset, and now dispersed to the nourishment of the travelling members of this Kingdome, &c. London, printed by W. S., Anno Domini 1611." Taylor had an especial grudge against Coryat, for having had influence enough to procure his "Laugh and be Fat"—directed against the traveller—to be burned; and that he never failed to "feed fat the ancient grudge," may be seen in the many pieces of ridicule levelled at the author of the "Crudities," even after his death.

[17] TOPHET.—The Hebrew name for *Hell*.

[18] CIMMERIAN.—Pertaining to the Cimmerii, or their country; extremely and perpetually dark. The Cimmerii were an ancient people of the land now called the Crimea, and their country being subject to heavy fogs, was fabled to be involved in deep and continual obscurity. Ancient poets also mention a people of this name who dwelt in a valley near Lake Avernus, in Italy, which the sun was said never to visit.

[19] PERTH.

[20] BRAEMAR.

[21] VIRGINAL JACK.—A keyed instrument resembling a spinet.

[22] RED-SHANKS.—A contemptuous appellation for Scottish Highland clansmen and native Irish, with reference to their naked hirsute limbs, and "As lively as a *Red-Shank*" is still a proverbial saying: —"And we came into Ireland, where they would have landed in the north parts. But I would not, because there the inhabitants were all *Red-shanks*."—*Sir Walter Raleigh's* Speech on the Scaffold.

[23] PUT ME INTO THAT SHAPE.—That is, invested him in Highland attire.

[24] "Probably the district around the skirts of Ben Muicdui."—*Chambers'* Domestic Annals of

Scotland.

[25] Balloch Castle.—Now called Castle-Grant.

[26] Moray.

[27] Morayland.

[28] Sugar-Candian.—*i.e.*, Sugar-candy.

[29] A Piece of Gold of Two-and-Twenty Shillings.—"This was a considerable present; but Jonson's hand and heart were ever open to his acquaintance. All his pleasures were social; and while health and fortune smiled upon him, he was no niggard either of his time or talents to those who needed them.   There is something striking in Taylor's concluding sentence, when the result of his (Jonson's) visit to Drummond is considered:—but there is one *evil that walks*, which keener eyes than John's have often failed to discover.— I have only to add, in justice to this honest man (Taylor) that his gratitude outlived the subject of it. He paid the tribute of a verse to his benefactor's memory:—the verse indeed, was   mean: but poor Taylor had nothing better to give."—Lt. Col. Francis Cunningham's edition of Gifford's Ben Jonson's Works, p. xli.

"In the summer of 1618 Scotland received a visit from the famous Ben Jonson. The burly Laureate walked all the way, among the motives for a journey then undertaken by few Englishmen, might be curiosity regarding a country from which he knew that his family was derived, his grandfather having been one of the Johnsons of Annandale. He had many friends too, particularly among the connections of the Lennox family, whom he might be glad to see at their own houses. Among those with whom he had amicable intercourse, was William Drummond, the poet, then in the prime of life, and living as a bachelor in his romantic mansion of Hawthornden, on the Esk, seven miles from Edinburgh. It is probable that Drummond and Jonson had met before in London, and indulged together in the "wit-combats" at the Mermaid and similar scenes. Indeed, there is a prevalent belief in Scotland that it was mainly to see Drummond at Hawthornden that Jonson came so far from home, and certain it is, from Drummond's report of his '*Conversations*,' that he designed 'to write a Fisher or Pastoral (Piscatory?) Play—and make the stage of it on the Lomond Lake—he also contemplated writing in prose his 'Foot Pilgrimage to Scotland,' which, with a feeling very natural in one who found so much to admire where so little had been known, he spoke of entitling 'A Discovery.' Unfortunately, this work, as well as a poem in which he called Edinburgh—

'The Heart of Scotland, Britain's other eye,'

has not been preserved to us. We can readily see that the work contemplated must have been of a general character, from Jonson's letters to Drummond on the subject of it. How much to be regretted that we have not the Scotland of that day delineated by so vigorous a pen as that of the author of *Sejanus*"— *Chambers'* Domestic Annals of Scotland, vol. 1.

Whether Taylor's "Penniless Pilgrimage" really did interfere with, and prevent the publication of Ben Jonson's 'Foot Pilgrimage' would now be difficult to say. It is very evident from Taylor's remarks in his Dedication "To all my loving adventurers, &c.," he had been accused by the critics that he "*did undergo this project, either in malice, or mockage of Master Benjamin Jonson*." It is quite certain that Taylor lost no time in getting his "Pilgrimage" printed "at the charges of the author" immediately on his return to London on the fifteenth of October 1618.

[30] Rouse.—A full glass, a bumper.

[31] Unfellowed.—*i.e.*, not matched.

[32] To Islington to the Sign of the Maindenhead.—This then roadside Public-house, we are informed from recent enquiries, was situate at the corner of Maiden Lane, Battle Bridge, now known as King's Cross, from a statue of George IV.—a most execrable performance taken down 1842. The "Old Pub" is turned into a gin palace, and named the Victoria, while Maiden Lane—an ancient way leading from Battle Bridge to Highgate Hill—is known now as York Road.

[33] Guy of Warwick.—There are several versions and editions of this work. In the book of the Stationers' Company, John Trundle—he at the sign of No-Body—on the 15th of January, 1619, entered "a play, called the Life and Death of Guy Earl of Warwick, written by John Day and Thomas Dekker."

43

See Baker's Biog. Dram., page 274, vol. 2.—"Well, if he read this with patience I'll be gelt, and troll ballads for Master Trundle yonder, the rest of my mortality."—*Ben Jonson's* Every Man in his Humour, act i. sc. 2.